First published in the United States
of America in 1990 by The Mallard Press

Mallard Press and its accompanying design
and logo are trademarks of BDD Promotional
Book Company, Inc.

Produced by
Twin Books
15 Sherwood Place
Greenwich, CT 06830

ISBN 0 792 45405 7

Printed in Hong Kong

Disney's MICKEY MOUSE
IN
BING BONG

Written by
Lee Nordling

TWIN BOOKS

MALLARD PRESS

Huge waves swept over the deck of the *Far, Far East*. Mickey Mouse, Minnie and Goofy were in the captain's quarters looking at a chart.

"Gawrsh, is that where we're going?" asked Goofy, pointing to a tiny dot added to the map in red ink. "Are you sure there's an island there?"

Mickey chuckled. "Sure, Goofy. Captain Huf discovered it."

"Fog Island wasn't on any known map," explained Captain Huf, "and I probably never would have found it if I hadn't made a wrong turn at Bali Hai."

"Well, Mick," said Goofy, "if it's not on any other map, isn't it sorta dangerous to go there?"

"Not really, Goofy," chuckled Mickey. "Besides, Captain Huf's friend, Chief Peasoup, needs our help."

"Oh, yeah," said Goofy. "There's some mysterious giant creature that's giving him trouble."

"Mysterious giant creature?" said Pete, who was listening from the engine room. "If there really is some kind of giant creature on that island, I could sell it to a zoo and make a pile of money!"

Three days later, the *Far, Far East* dropped anchor at Fog Island. "I can't see a thing," said Goofy.

"That's why the natives call it Fog Island," said Captain Huf, as Mickey and Goofy rowed the gang ashore. Pete followed in another rowboat.

11

"Welcome to Fog Island," said Chief Peasoup to his visitors. "Won't you join us for dinner? The carrot is almost done."

"You poor dears!" said Minnie. "All you have is a carrot?"

"Well, it's a pretty big one," laughed the Chief, as four men arrived with a ten-foot cooked carrot.

"Wow!" said Mickey. "Things do grow big here. What can you tell us about your mysterious giant creature?"

"We've never seen him, said the Chief, "but we call him Bing Bong because he moves so fast that the wind chimes ring when he comes to steal one of our giant carrots."

"We'll get to the bottom of this for you, Chief," said Mickey.

"Please be careful," said Chief Peasoup. "And this young lady should stay away from Bing Bong!"

"But why?" asked Minnie.

"In those orange clothes, you look like a carrot!"

"Oh, Chief," giggled Minnie. "Surely this Bing Bong can tell the difference between me and a carrot!"

The four friends waved good-bye and went into the jungle. Within an hour, they were hopelessly lost.

And what a place to be lost in! They were chased by forty-foot snakes, giant apes, and the fiercest dinosaur ever — *Tyrannosaurus rex*!

The *Tyrannosaurus* lurched forward, its tongue darting out between long, pointed teeth. Mickey stood his ground bravely with a handmade spear.

The dinosaur reared back, roared its challenge, then swept Mickey aside and snapped at Minnie. But before it could strike again, it was attacked by the oddest creature Mickey had even seen: a giant saber-toothed bunny!

Amazed, Mickey, Minnie, Captain Huf and Goofy watched the battle of the titans—bunny versus dinosaur. Suddenly, they realized this was their chance to escape.

"Let's get out of here!" cried Mickey. "It sounds like the winner may come to claim his lunch!" Before long they heard the rustling of bushes behind them!

They stumbled into the clearing before the Fog Island village. Halfway to the gate, the ground started to shake. Turning, they saw the fifty-foot bunny bounding from the bushes.

The saber-toothed bunny leaped over their heads and landed between them and the gate. Chief Peasoup waved wildly for them to hurry. The bunny reared up on its hind legs and beat its chest with its furry paws. Then it crouched and sprang again. As it passed over their heads, it nipped at Minnie's hat.

"I warned you to be careful what you wore!" shouted Chief Peasoup. "That must be Bing Bong. He wants his carrot!"

"Quick!" shouted Mickey. They ran through the gate and found themselves in a giant bamboo cage. As they turned, they saw Bing Bong almost on top of them.

Mickey, Minnie, Captain Huf and Goofy squeezed out of the cage between the heavy bamboo bars. The gate slid down and the giant bunny was trapped.

"Har, har, har!" Pete laughed from the top of the cage.

"Pete!" said Mickey. "Where did you come from?"

"I signed on with Captain Huf's crew," said Pete. "But now I have the ship, the bunny, and you!"

It didn't take long for Mickey to discover what had happened. Pete had forced the natives to build the cage that caught Bing Bong. Now that the giant bunny had been captured, Pete turned on Mickey and his friends and tied them up.

Pete floated the cage to the ship and stowed it in the hold. He untied Mickey, Minnie, Goofy and Captain Huf and threw them into the hold, too.

"Poor Bing Bong," said Minnie, gazing at the giant rabbit. "He looks so unhappy!"

Pete laughed down at them from the deck. "So what?" he snarled. "People will pay to see him, whether he's happy or not!" And he slammed the hatch cover shut.

Several days later, Minnie was still worried about Bing Bong. She knelt next to the cage and stroked the bunny's nose. "Don't be sad, Bing Bong," she said. "We'll help you."

"We can't even help ourselves right now," Mickey pointed out. "I don't know how we're going to help Bing Bong."

"Oh, Mickey," pleaded Minnie. "We have to do something! He wants to go home."

I'd turn this boat around and take him home right now," said Captain Huf, "if I weren't a prisoner on my own ship!"

The big bunny sniffed and blinked back a tear. "I can't stand it!" cried Minnie. "Isn't there any way we can get him out of this cage?"

Get him out...Goofy thought to himself. Hmmm...

Tugboats brought the *Far, Far East* into New York Harbor and up the Hudson River, guiding it safely to the dock. On deck, Pete had opened the main hatch and was waiting at the gangway for permission to unload his cargo.

Suddenly, one of the sailors let out a yell: "Bunny off the port bow!"

Pete turned to see Bing Bong leaping from the deck to the dock, then bounding over buildings toward downtown and the skyscrapers.

Pete was stunned. "What happened?" he asked.

Goofy popped his head up from the hold and said, "Minnie wanted him out of his cage, so I opened it!"

The harbormaster rushed up the gangplank, flanked by two policemen. They backed Pete up against a wall. "Was that your bunny that just jumped ship without clearing customs?" demanded the harbormaster.

Pete looked from one policeman to the other and said, "Oh, no, sir! I'm just part of the crew."

"He's lying," said Mickey, climbing out of the hold. "He *is* the one you want. He kidnapped that bunny and brought him to New York."

As the policemen led Pete away, Mickey told the harbormaster what had happened, and promised to recapture Bing Bong.

Leaving Captain Huf and Goofy with the ship, Mickey and Minnie hailed a cab. "Follow that bunny!" cried Mickey.

Bing Bong was certainly a sight to see—a towering, long-eared mass of white fluff hopping down the street as if he were late for an important meeting.

"He looks so scared!" said Minnie. "He doesn't understand where he is or why people are honking at him!"

They caught up with Bing Bong back at the harbor, but suddenly, he leaped onto a moving ferry.

Mickey and Minnie borrowed a speedboat and streaked after Bing Bong and the ferry. Mickey got Captain Huf on the radio and said, "Bring your ship to Liberty Island! Bing Bong is trying to find his way home by any boat he can!"

"Aye, aye, Mickey," said Captain Huf. "See you there!"

Once the ferry came within distance of Liberty Island, Bing Bong leaped ashore and looked around. Nothing looked right. This wasn't home. Then he looked up and hopped with delight. A very tall creature was holding what looked like a very big carrot.

"He's climbing up the Statue of Liberty!" cried Mickey.

When Bing Bong reached the shoulders of the statue, he sniffed at the torch. He was disappointed—it wasn't a carrot, after all.

Mickey and Minnie were met at the dock by a guard. "We have to get that creature down!" said the guard.

Mickey saw Bing Bong sniffing the torch. "I have an idea," he said.

"You'd better do something quick," said the guard. "Four helicopters are on their way!"

Just then Captain Huf and Goofy arrived on the *Far, Far East*.

Moments later, the helicopters began to buzz Bing Bong.

Minnie gasped as the helicopters swooped toward the bunny. "No!" she cried.

Bing Bong cringed away to avoid the attack and began to lose his balance. He grabbed hold of Liberty's torch and held on tightly, his eyes squeezed shut.

Mickey called to Captain Huf, "Quickly! Unload as many giant carrots as you can!"

Captain Huf and Goofy went to work and soon had dumped several large bunches of carrots at the base of the statue.

Mickey turned to Minnie and said, "Do you know what to do?" Minnie nodded.

Over the roar of the helicopter blades, Bing Bong heard his name called. His sensitive ears recognized the voice.

"Bing Bong! Bing Bong!" cried Minnie. "Oh, please come down and have a carrot! We'll take you home! I promise we will!"

The saber-toothed bunny looked down and saw Minnie standing next to the pile of giant carrots.

That's when Bing Bong leaped off the Statue of Liberty! It was the mightiest leap he had ever made. He soared far out over their heads and splashed into the harbor. Then he turned around, swam to shore, shook the water from his fur and hopped to Minnie's open arms.

Soon they all set out again for Fog Island. They radioed Chief Peasoup that they were bringing Bing Bong back.

"Oh, thank goodness!" he said. "Ever since that nasty Pete took him away, we've been overrun with dinosaurs! Bing Bong was the only thing big enough to keep them away from the village!"

"How did you know Bing Bong would come down for a carrot?" Goofy asked Mickey, as they sat with Minnie in the hold of the ship, watching the giant bunny.

"It wasn't the carrot he came down for," said Mickey, looking fondly at Minnie. "It was Minnie. I think he was just as hungry for her affection as he was for the carrot."

At that point, as if on cue, Bing Bong reached over and gave Minnie a giant saber-toothed kiss.